Put Beginning Readers on the Right Track with ALL ABOARD READING™

The All Aboard Reading series is especially designed for beginning readers. Written by noted authors and illustrated in full color, these are books that children really want to read—books to excite their imagination, expand their interests, make them laugh, and support their feelings. With fiction and nonfiction stories that are high interest and curriculum-related, All Aboard Reading books offer something for every young reader. And with four different reading levels, the All Aboard Reading series lets you choose which books are most appropriate for your children and their growing abilities.

Picture Readers
Picture Readers have super-simple texts, with many nouns appearing as rebus pictures. At the end of each book are 24 flash cards—on one side is a rebus picture; on the other side is the written-out word.

Station Stop 1
Station Stop 1 books are best for children who have just begun to read. Simple words and big type make these early reading experiences more comfortable. Picture clues help children to figure out the words on the page. Lots of repetition throughout the text helps children to predict the next word or phrase—an essential step in developing word recognition.

Station Stop 2
Station Stop 2 books are written specifically for children who are reading with help. Short sentences make it easier for early readers to understand what they are reading. Simple plots and simple dialogue help children with reading comprehension.

Station Stop 3
Station Stop 3 books are perfect for children who are reading alone. With longer text and harder words, these books appeal to children who have mastered basic reading skills. More complex stories captivate children who are ready for more challenging books.

In addition to All Aboard Reading books, look for All Aboard Math Readers™ (fiction stories that teach math concepts children are learning in school); All Aboard Science Readers™ (nonfiction books that explore the most fascinating science topics in age-appropriate language); All Aboard Poetry Readers™ (funny, rhyming poems for readers of all levels); and All Aboard Mystery Readers™ (puzzling tales where children piece together evidence with the characters).

All Aboard for happy reading!

GROSSET & DUNLAP
Published by the Penguin Group
Penguin Group (USA) Inc., 375 Hudson Street, New York, New York 10014, USA
Penguin Group (Canada), 90 Eglinton Avenue East, Suite 700, Toronto,
Ontario M4P 2Y3, Canada (a division of Pearson Penguin Canada Inc.)
Penguin Books Ltd., 80 Strand, London WC2R 0RL, England
Penguin Group Ireland, 25 St. Stephen's Green, Dublin 2, Ireland
(a division of Penguin Books Ltd.)
Penguin Group (Australia), 250 Camberwell Road, Camberwell, Victoria 3124,
Australia (a division of Pearson Australia Group Pty. Ltd.)
Penguin Books India Pvt. Ltd., 11 Community Centre, Panchsheel Park,
New Delhi—110 017, India
Penguin Group (NZ), 67 Apollo Drive, Rosedale, North Shore 0632, New Zealand
(a division of Pearson New Zealand Ltd.)
Penguin Books (South Africa) (Pty.) Ltd., 24 Sturdee Avenue,
Rosebank, Johannesburg 2196, South Africa

Penguin Books Ltd., Registered Offices: 80 Strand, London WC2R 0RL, England

Paperback ISBN 978-0-448-45220-3   10 9 8 7 6 5 4 3 2 1
Hardcover ISBN 978-0-448-45226-5   10 9 8 7 6 5 4 3 2 1

Super WHY

Hansel and Gretel

Based on the television series *Super WHY!*,
created by Angela C. Santomero, as seen on PBS KIDS

Text based on the script written
by Angela C. Santomero and Jennifer Hamburg.

Adapted by Samantha Brooke   Cover Illustration by MJ Illustrations

Grosset & Dunlap

Red Riding Hood
has a problem.
At the Book Club,
she tells the Super Readers,
"I ate Peter Piper's peppers.
He is mad. What can I do?"

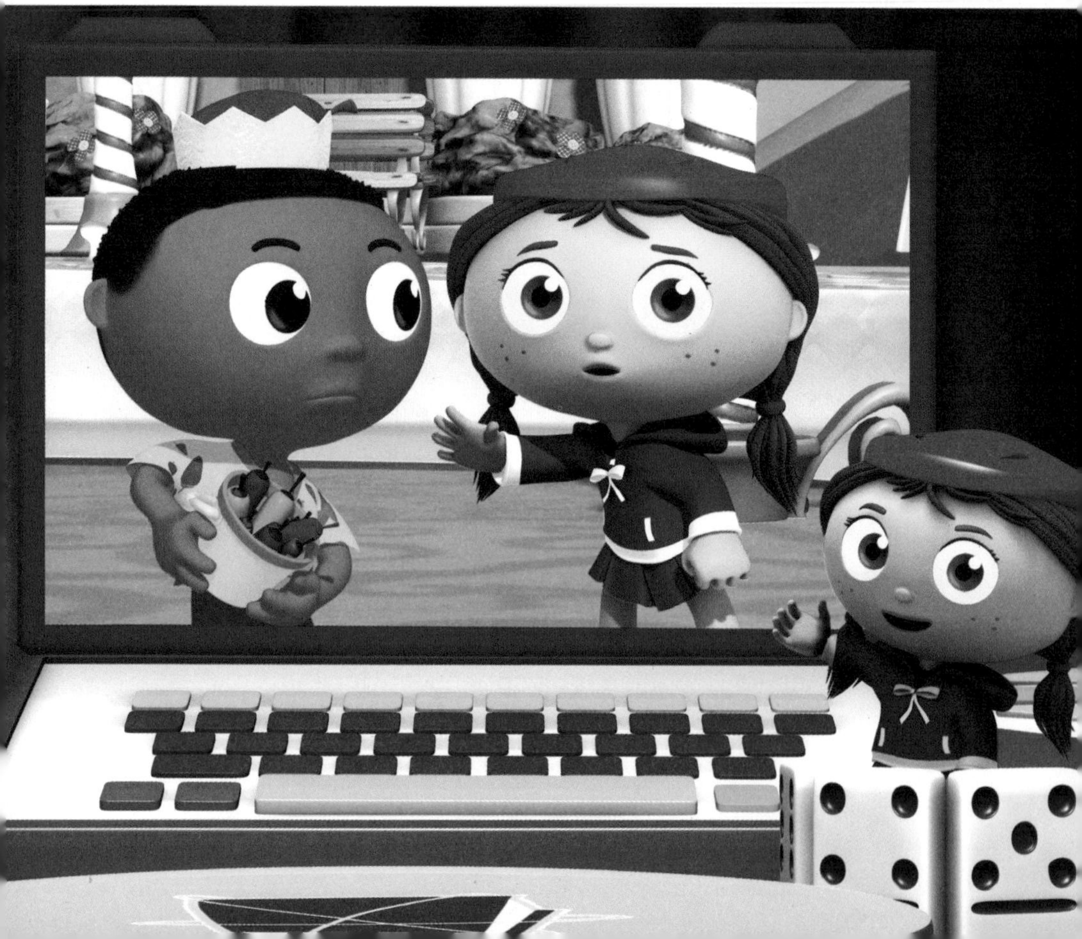

Whyatt says,

"When we have a problem,

we look in a book."

Princess Pea waves
her magic wand.
She says,
"Peas and carrots,
carrots and peas,
book come out,
please, please, please!"

A book flies off the shelf.

The title is *Hansel and Gretel*.

In a flash of stars,
the Super Readers
change into
super heroes.

Alpha Pig with Alphabet Power!

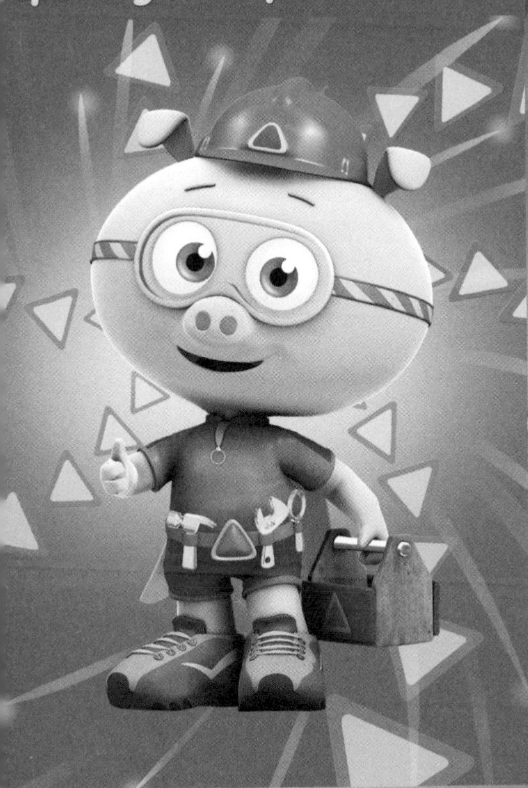

WONDER RED WITH WORD POWER!

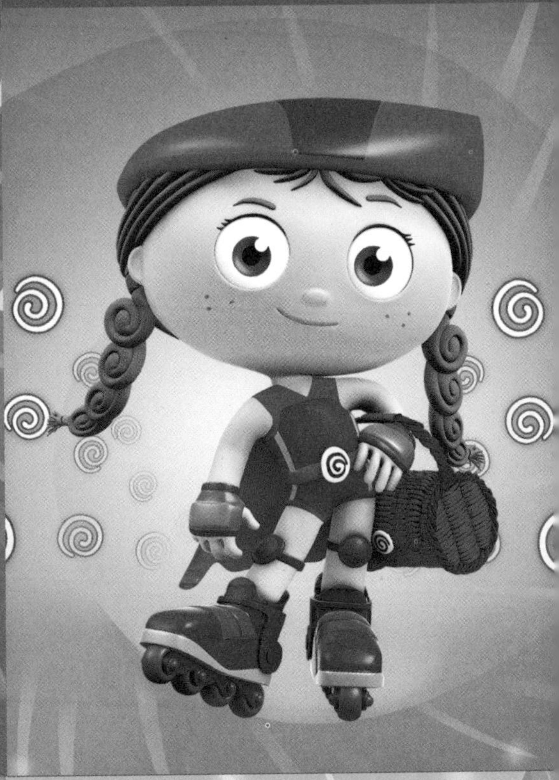

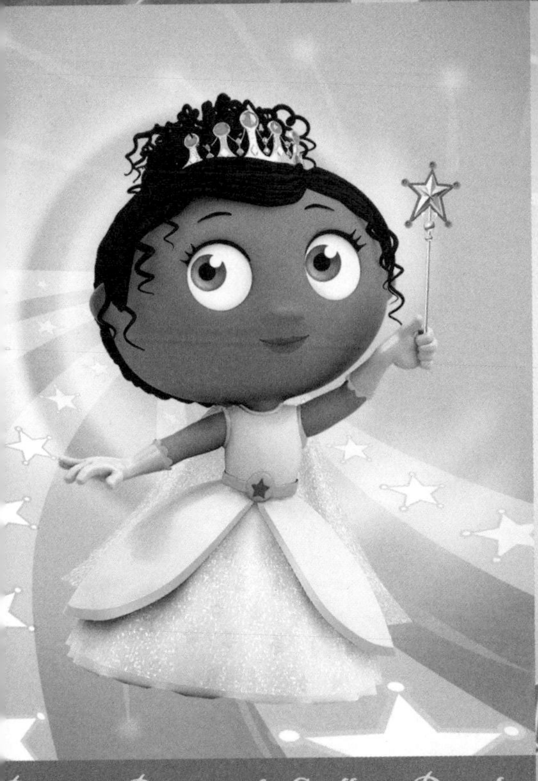

Princess Presto with Spelling Power!

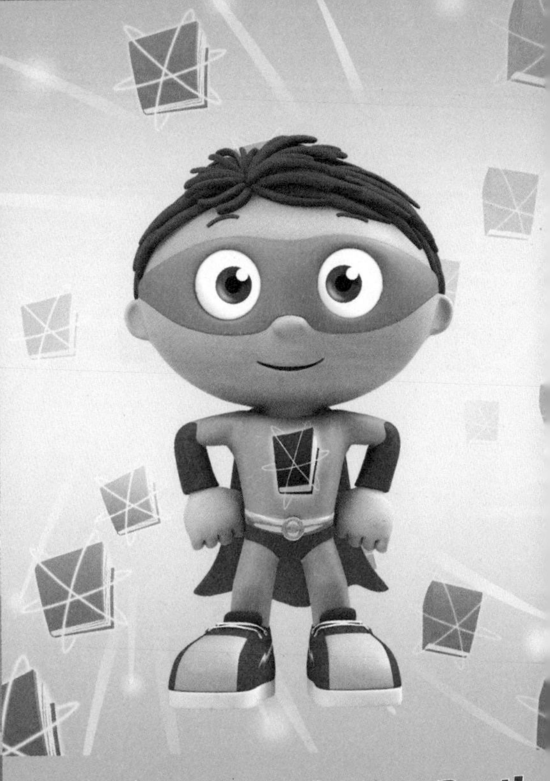

Super Why with the Power to Read!

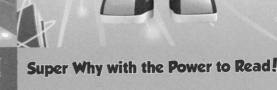

They climb into their
Why Flyers and say,
"Super Readers . . . to the rescue!"
Then they fly into the book.

Princess Presto says,
"In this book,
Hansel and Gretel eat
the witch's cookie house.
She gets very mad."

Wonder Red says,
"The witch is mad,
just like Peter Piper is mad."

Alpha Pig says,
"We need to talk
to the witch!"

Alpha Pig says,
"I see the witch's house.
It is across this river.
Oh no! How can we
cross this river?"

Princess Presto says,

"I can make a raft."

She uses her

Magic Spelling Wand.

She spells <u>raft</u>.

"R-A-F-T. Presto!"

The Super Readers
hop on the raft.
They cross the river.

"Look! I see
Hansel and Gretel,"
says Super Why.

Hansel and Gretel
each take a bite of the
witch's cookie roof.

The witch comes out.
"You ate my roof!
What will I do
if it rains?" she cries.

The witch is very mad.
She goes into her house,
then slams the door!

Hansel says, "Oh no!"
Gretel says, "We cannot
talk to the witch if her
door is closed."

Super Why says,

"We can help you."

Gretel asks,

"How? Our story says,

'The witch closes the door.'"

The witch closes the door.

Super Why says,
"I can change the story,
so you can talk to the witch."

Super Why changes
the sentence.
He takes out the word <u>closes</u>.
He puts in the word <u>opens</u>.
Zzzap!

opens

The witch closes the door.

The witch opens the door.

The witch opens the door.
Hurray!
Now Hansel and Gretel
can talk to her.

"We are sorry for
eating your gingerbread
cookie house,"
Hansel tells the witch.

"Next time we will ask first,"
says Gretel.
The witch says, "Thank you."
Hansel says, "You do make
great cookie houses."
The witch has an idea!

The witch says,
"Look! I made little
cookie houses."

"May we have one?"
asks Gretel.
The witch says, "Yes.
Thank you for asking."

The Super Readers fly home.

Red finds Peter Piper.

She wants to say

she is sorry.

Red says, "I am sorry
I took your peppers
without asking, Peter."
Peter says, "Thanks, Red.
I still have some peppers."
Red says, "Can I please
have one?"
Peter says, "Yes!"

"Hip, hip, hurray! The Super Readers saved the day!
We changed the story. We solved the problem.
We worked together so . . .
Hip, hip, hurray! The Super Readers saved the day!"